Books by Robert Bright

The Friendly Bear

Georgie

Georgie and the Robbers

Georgie to the Rescue

Georgie's Halloween

Georgie and the Magician

Georgie and the Noisy Ghost

I Like Red

Me and the Bears

My Hopping Bunny

Richard Brown and the Dragon

Which Is Willy?

Gregory

Weekly Reader Children's Book Club presents

Georgie Goes West

by ROBERT BRIGHT

Doubleday & Company, Inc.

Garden City, New York

ISBN: 0-385-05271-5 TRADE
       0-385-05277-4 PREBOUND
Library of Congress Catalog Card Number 73-79650
Copyright © 1973 by Robert Bright
All Rights Reserved
Printed in the United States of America
Published by arrangement with Doubleday & Co., Inc.

Weekly Reader Children's Book Club Edition

FOR KATHERINE

Now everybody knows that the pioneers went West
in covered wagons drawn by horses. But when the
Whittakers went West they did better. Because
Mr. Whittaker built a sturdy little house on their
automobile, and that made it cozy for them while they
traveled.

But for Georgie it was special. Because that little
house had a little attic. And what little ghost could
resist an attic that rolled on wheels?

So Georgie and his little friends, Herman the cat and
Miss Oliver the owl, went rolling along and it was almost
like home.

That is, until they got to the BIG COUNTRY
of the high mountains and the broad
plains. And that country was beautiful.
But Georgie could see it was much too big
for a little ghost.

Just the same, Miss Oliver looked for a little bird that chirped. But a big eagle swooped down on her and screamed.

Herman thought he'd find a little kitty-cat that mewed.
But a big wildcat pounced on him and snarled.

Georgie thought surely there would
be a harmless cow that mooed. But
hundreds of cows came after him
like thunder and they bellowed.

Then Georgie knew the West wasn't only
too big but it was much too exciting for a little
ghost, and he was thankful that at least
the Whittakers were peaceable and of
an ordinary size.

That is, until they bought their big exciting
western outfits with high boots and tall hats.
Georgie felt so little he decided he'd just have to
mope in his attic for the rest of the trip.

But when Mr. Whittaker drove
into an Indian village Georgie was so
curious he just had to take a peek.

It was a lucky thing he did. Because that's when he saw
the unhappy little Indian boy. His name was Kio and Georgie
thought he was unhappy because he was so little.

But Herman, who had been around listening, said that the trouble was horse thieves. They had come at dawn and stolen the best horses. And that was bad. But they had taken Kio's pinto—Little Lightning. And that was worse. Because Kio and Little Lightning loved each other and they would never be happy until they were together again.

All day the big exciting people had been looking for those horse thieves. The Indians were looking. The cowboys were looking. The sheriff was looking.

EVERYBODY was helping.

Then Mr. Whittaker decided he'd help too. He got off to such a fast start he almost left everybody else behind.

He drove straight up the side of a mountain.

He was so excited it was a wonder he didn't fall off.

Maybe he would have if all his tires hadn't gone flat and his radiator hadn't blown its cap. Besides night had come on and you couldn't chase horse thieves in the dark.

Everywhere else they were giving up the chase for the night.
The sheriff rode back to the jail; the cowboys rode back
to the chuck wagon; the Indians rode back to the village.
And they all thought the same thing—that the horse
thieves had gotten clean away.

Kio thought so and wanted to cry. But Indians aren't supposed to cry.

Mr. and Mrs. Whittaker thought so and felt so bad they couldn't go to sleep.

The horse thieves thought so but they went to sleep
smiling to themselves. Because if the Indians
and the cowboys and the sheriff couldn't find them
in the day, who could find them at night?

Well Georgie thought somebody could. He and his little friends, Herman and Miss Oliver, had a little talk about it.

First Miss Oliver did a lot of flying around, and with her
night eyes she could see everything as clear as day. That's
how she spotted the horse thieves

and saw Little Lightning tied to a little tree.

Now a little owl could find Little Lightning. But it took a clever little cat with his clever little paws and his sharp little teeth to untie him.

And maybe a little ghost couldn't jump
on a horse. But he could float up like a balloon.

Now Georgie had never ridden a horse. He had never even
ridden a harmless cow. But tonight Georgie rode Little
Lightning down the mountain

and across the plain.

Georgie rode right up to Kio's front door.
And what a joyous meeting that was!
But Georgie warned Kio there was not time to
lose if they wanted to catch the horse thieves.

With one leap Kio was on Little Lightning with Georgie and they woke up the Indians—

and they woke up the sheriff

and they woke up the cowboys

and they all rode into the mountains

and captured the horse thieves.

and the cowboys hauled the Whittakers back to the town.

Now the sheriff took the horse thieves to the jail,

the Indians took their horses back to the village,

But Kio took Georgie to his favorite tree and
gave him a fine feather bonnet.

Georgie was so proud he'd never felt
so proud before.

Then Herman felt so pleased he
jumped higher than a wildcat
and he'd never jumped so high before.

But Miss Oliver flew higher than
an eagle and
she said

And she'd never said *THAT* before.

Robert Bright was born on Cape Cod, spent his childhood in Europe, and completed his education at Phillips Academy, Andover, and Princeton University.

His vocations include those of newspaper reporter in Baltimore and Paris, art and music critic in Santa Fe, New Mexico, teacher in Boston, and novelist. Believing that "the imaginative child in the imaginative man is fortunately never far away," Mr. Bright has delighted in writing and illustrating his fourteen books for children. Six of these star Georgie, the friendly little ghost who first appeared in 1944 and who has been charming young readers on both sides of the Atlantic ever since.

Robert Bright has his center in Santa Fe, but becomes nomadic during winters and springs. The happy stimulus for the earliest Georgie books furnished by his children, Beatrice and Robin, is now provided by two handy grandsons, Michael and Christopher.